W9-BGK-463

JOHN D. MacDONALD
"One of our best craftsmen!"
The San Francisco Chronicle

JOHN D. MacDONALD
"A masterful writer!"
The Chicago Tribune

JOHN D. MacDONALD
"An expert storyteller!"
The New York Times

JOHN D. MacDONALD
"The best novelist in America!"
Pete Hamill, *The New York Daily News*

Fawcett Gold Medal Books
by John D. MacDonald

All These Condemned
April Evil
Area of Suspicion
Barrier Island
The Beach Girls
Border Town Girl
The Brass Cupcake
A Bullet for Cinderella
Cancel All Our Vows
Clemmie
Condominium
Contrary Pleasure
The Crossroads
Cry Hard, Cry Fast
The Damned
Dead Low Tide
Deadly Welcome
Death Trap
The Deceivers
The Drowner
The Empty Trap
The End of the Night
End of the Tiger and Other Stories
The Executioners
A Flash of Green
The Girl, the Gold Watch and Everything
The Good Old Stuff
Judge Me Not
A Key to the Suite
The Last One Left
A Man of Affairs
Murder for the Bride
Murder in the Wind
The Neon Jungle
Nothing Can Go Wrong
One Monday We Killed Them All
One More Sunday
On the Run
The Only Girl in the Game
Please Write For Details
The Price of Murder
Seven
Slam the Big Door
Soft Touch
Where is Janice Gantry?
You Live Once

TRAVIS McGEE SERIES

Bright Orange for the Shroud
Cinnamon Skin
Darker Than Amber
A Deadly Shade of Gold
The Deep Blue Good-By
The Dreadful Lemon Sky
Dress Her in Indigo
The Empty Copper Sea
Free Fall in Crimson
The Girl in the Plain Brown Wrapper
The Green Ripper
The Lonely Silver Rain
The Long Lavender Look
Nightmare in Pink
Official Travis McGee Quizbook
One Fearful Yellow Eye
Pale Gray for Guilt
A Purple Place for Dying
The Quick Red Fox
The Scarlet Ruse
A Tan and Sandy Silence
The Turquoise Lament

JOHN D. MACDONALD

THE EMPTY TRAP

FAWCETT GOLD MEDAL • NEW YORK

A Fawcett Gold Medal Book
Published by Ballantine Books

Copyright © 1957 by John D. MacDonald

All rights reserved under International and Pan-American Copyright Conventions, including the right to reproduce this book or portions thereof. Published in the United States by Ballantine Books, a division of Random House, Inc., New York, and simultaneously in Canada by Random House of Canada Limited, Toronto.

All characters in this book are fictional and any resemblance to persons living or dead is purely coincidental.

ISBN 0-449-12854-7

Printed in Canada

First Fawcett Gold Medal Edition: April 1962
First Ballantine Books Edition: June 1983
Third Printing: July 1987

THE EMPTY TRAP

1

The clouds were low over the mountains. The two cars had climbed the graveled road up out of the night into the first light of dawn. At times there would be a break in the cloud level and through them he could see the brown peaks above timberline touched with the gold and pink of the rising sun.

He was in the lead car, the dark blue Chrysler with Nevada plates. Tulsa Haynes drove slowly, big hands on the wheel. The world had been black shadows, with yellow headlights moving cautiously ahead. Now first light brought color into the world, a bronze to the backs of Tulsa's hands, a blue gleam to the car hood. Tulsa turned the lights off and, moments later, the lights of the Pontiac that followed closely went off and the two cars moved up the mountain curves of the grey road.

He was in the middle, between Tulsa and Valerez. He sat awkwardly, wrists bound behind him, ankles lashed together, both tied tightly with a sheer nylon stocking, gossamer thin, unbreakably strong. Valerez, at Tulsa's order, had unknotted the gag shortly after they had driven away from the Motel Montañas, had pulled the strip of toweling out of Lloyd's mouth and dropped it out the side window. It was cold up in the dawn mountains. He could smell the dried acid of the perspiration on his clothing, the sweat of pain and fear. And he could smell the stink of his burned chest.

Valerez had just lighted another cigarette. Back in the motel Lloyd had seen the name on the packet. Delicados. Valerez held the cigarette to Lloyd's lips. The paper had a sugary taste. The smoke was raw and strong when he sucked it down into his lungs.

Tulsa had been going more slowly, watching the drop at the right side of the road. He stopped. "You think it's okay, Giz?"

"It is wild country. But we should look, maybe."

Tulsa turned off the motor, took the key out, set the parking brake hard. Lloyd knew he took no chances. At no time had he left any opening. He was a professional. They got out and walked up ahead of the car, walked fifty feet. Benny, who had been driving the Pontiac, hurried to join them. There was no need for Benny to take precautions. Sylvia, his only passenger, was dead.

Lloyd Wescott watched them. They pointed over the drop. It was very still in the mountains, with no sound of bird or insect. They talked together and he could not hear them. Tulsa stood with his big hands on his hips. Had he not been beside the others, his breadth of shoulder would have made him look shorter than his six feet. He wore tailored khakis, skin-tight at the waist, taut around lean hips. The short stiff black hair was like a cap, and when the sun broke through, Lloyd saw a pink highlight on Tulsa's quarter profile, on the high hard cheekbone. Benny, the squat little man with the clown face, pranced and gesticulated as he talked. Valerez, the stranger, had put his dark suit coat on over the pink shirt, the dark maroon knit tie with the ruby pin. His black hair gleamed above the pale, narrow, handsome face, and he stood a little apart from the other two.

Careful selection of grave, Lloyd thought. And I can be grateful to them for one thing. There isn't any room in me for fear, or regret or remorse. No room for anything but hate. Life ends here. The lights go out. I should be thinking about eternity, and remembering, in this last time left to me, all the bright days of my life. And all I can think about is how I want to see them dead.

Tulsa made a gesture of impatience, of decision, then sent Benny back to the Pontiac. Tulsa returned to the Chrysler, leaned on the window frame on the driver's side and looked in at Lloyd.

"I'll make it easy," he said.

"Thanks." The word was blurred by Lloyd's broken mouth.

"You got more guts than I figured, boy. Harry said make it rough for both of you. She got it rough. But the way I figure, she knew what she was doing, and you got suckered along. This wasn't your league, Lloyd. So I'll make it easy. You won't know about it."

"Don't . . . do me any favors."

"I'll let Harry know you took it good. And she took it bad."

Benny swung the Pontiac around the Chrysler, brought it to a precise stop aimed at an angle toward the drop. Tulsa said to Valerez, "How soon before anybody finds them?"

"One cannot say. A week, a month, maybe one hour. But it does not matter."

"What the hell do you mean?"

"These people, you think they call the policia? There will be things of value, perhaps pieces of the car to be taken to a village, sold for a few centavos."

Tulsa snapped his thick fingers. "God damn. I nearly forgot. Harry woulda chewed me good. Benny!"

"Yeah?"

"Get those rings off her."

"Rings? Sure." He dived back into the Pontiac. After a few moments he called to Tulsa, "They're on tight."

"Those rings are worth three grand," Tulsa said. "Harry told me before he married her."

"Thirty-six thousand pesos," Valerez said wistfully.

Benny came back with the rings and gave them to Tulsa. Benny looked in brightly at Lloyd. "How they breaking, pal?"

"Cut his ankles loose, Giz," Tulsa said. Valerez leaned in and, with quick blade thrust, deftly slit the nylon at his ankles. Tulsa pulled him out the other side of the car and set him on his feet. Lloyd's knees sagged. Tulsa cursed and bent as though to carry him over his shoulder. Lloyd felt there might be one slim chance if he kept on his feet. Not a chance to save himself. It had gone far beyond that.

"Can walk," he said, and locked his knees. The pain of the burned feet was excruciating.

"A gutsy guy," Benny said admiringly. "He maybe was in the wrong business, Tuls."

They held his arms, Tulsa on his left, Benny on his right, and walked him toward the Pontiac. He walked as steadily and as strongly as he could, forcing himself with what was left of strength and will. Tulsa did not relax his hold, but Benny did. He felt the slackening of the grip. He timed his steps, summoned up the last bit of explosive energy in deadened muscles, then lunged hard to his right. Tulsa hauled him back. But his shoulder had slammed hard into Benny's. Benny lost his grip and staggered toward the brink, giving a shrill yelp of fright. He fell, scrabbling at the gravel, half over, sliding further, yelling again. Valerez reached him at the last instant, caught his wrist. They were both poised there and Lloyd tried to dive at them, to take both of them over with him, but Tulsa held him. All energy gone, Lloyd sagged to his knees. Valerez pulled Benny back onto the road. Benny sat, his face grey, cursing thickly. He got up slowly, came over and kicked Lloyd in the side.

"God damn, Tuls," he said. "I'm shakin' all over. Jesus!" He kicked Lloyd again, heavily.

"Cut it out," Tulsa said. "Get him on his feet."

"I've always been scared of falling off something high."

When they stood him up, Lloyd thought he wouldn't be able to speak, but he managed to say, "Then . . . that's the . . . way you're . . . going to die . . . Benny."

"What the hell do you mean?"

"Everybody . . . dies the way . . . they're scared of."

"Hey, is he kiddin' me, Tuls? Is he?"

"Shut up. Get the door open there."

Tulsa put him in the car, behind the wheel. Sylvia was slumped against the door on the far side, body slack in death, black hair wreathing the side of the empurpled face. Benny had dressed her after death, dressed her in the yellow short-sleeved sweater, the pistachio flannel skirt. Tulsa gave an order, and Valerez and Benny Bernholz went over the car, wiping it clean.

"When I say go, push with your shoulders," he said. "Don't touch it."

Tulsa reached a heavy arm through the window, a spring-handled sap in his hand. "This'll make it easier," he said. He snapped the lead end of the sap against Lloyd's forehead with a backhanded twist of his wrist. Lloyd moved instinctively, and just quickly enough so that it glanced off the side of his forehead, just ahead of the temple. One of the familiar pain-flowers bloomed and burst in gaudy blue and white and at the other end of an echoing tunnel he heard Tulsa yell, "Push!"

He could not move, but he could see straight ahead. "Wait," Tulsa yelled and he held the car back with his great strength. Lloyd was only partially aware when Valerez reached in, cut the nylon from his wrists. Again they pushed. The car moved forward. The right front corner dropped first. It happened so very slowly. Now, he thought, that thing they talk about is happening!

I argued with the salesman about this car, about his offer. The red and white hardtop convertible. He wanted fourteen hundred difference and I wanted to trade for a thousand. When I went into the sales manager's office, the air conditioning was turned very low. There was an award certificate on the wall. We could not get anywhere until I told him I was the manager at the Hotel Green Oasis, and then the atmosphere was more cordial and we traded for eleven fifty and I drove it back, and it smelled new and it ran well, and that was the week Harry Danton brought Sylvia back from Los Angeles and they moved into the hotel.

It dropped on the right side, and he was thrown against Sylvia's body and for one moment he could look down the long cruel slant of steep brown rock, at small wiry trees that grew out of the rock, and then the roll and fall continued a clanging and crashing and a steep sickness, and then he spun high and free and he saw the car and the mountains turn around him and knew he was apart from the car. Then, in the turn, the brown rocks came up to a smash of whiteness against his face, a floodlight whiteness that dwindled down and away like the last white spot on a cooling TV picture tube.

He knew he was cold. There were great sounds around him. It was very difficult to think. Needles of cold beat against his face. He turned his face slowly and with great difficulty until his cheek touched a sharp edge. He opened his eyes and he saw wet rock inches from his eyes. The rain drove against wet rock, exploding into silvery mist. There was a blue glare of lightning and then thunder cracked loudly and the long echoes boomed and rolled through the mountains. Slowly he began to know that he was bent oddly, body arched back at the waist, something hard across the small of his back. Lightning was close for a long time, and then moved away and the rain slackened and stopped. He felt rigid with cold. Almost at once the sun came out, a high white glare over the mountains, and the wet rocks began to steam. He could not think why he was here, where this place was, why he should be made so uncomfortable. When he tried to move pain brought a threatening blackness. His right hand and arm seemed willing to move when he willed it. He brought his right hand up close to his face. He turned his hand over and looked with distant curiosity, with a clinical remoteness, at the great tear in the heel of his palm, at the thick flap of skin and flesh that lay back over his wrist. It bled slowly.

Inch by painful inch he turned his body to the right, toward the cliff face, moving his face back from the corner of rock. The hardness that had been across his back now bit into his waist. After another few inches he turned the rest of the way suddenly and the hard thing was across his belly and he was jackknifed across it. And he looked down a steep sickening slant. There was brown rock and sun on steaming brown rock, and a few trees with knotted trunks no bigger than his forearm. Far below him he saw a patch of color, of red and white. He closed his eyes. The height made him feel sick. When he could look again, he knew it was the car. His car. His mind and memory until that moment had been like a dry stream bed. The single act of recognition of the car was like opening a dam at the head of the stream. The waters came roaring down, turbulent, filling it from brim to brim.

He closed his eyes again. Blood pounded in his head. Have to think, he told himself. Hanging across a tree. Broken all to hell. Thrown clear. Ought to be dead. Can very easily become dead. Just wiggle a little. Slide off the tree. Never feel a thing after the first bounce.

But it would be nice to see Tulsa Haynes. And Benny Bernholz. And Giz Valerez. And Harry Danton. Maybe, most of all, Harry Danton.

He felt as though the tree was slowly cutting him in half. He could see his legs, ankles, feet. Both shoes were gone. His left foot was twisted crazily to the side, the ankle big as a melon. Blood dripped from the toes of the right foot. He tried to swallow and could not. His entire face felt numb below the eyes. He touched his face with the fingers of his right hand. He could not identify what he felt. Bone in the wrong place. Splintered things that could be teeth. He let the right arm hang. He wept for himself, wept for the broken body. This was the gateway to death; he was a half step away.

He felt unconsciousness coming, the way a night shadow moves across a lawn. He fought it back. He looked down again. There was the steep drop. Close below the tree was a ledge. It was more of a crevasse than a ledge. The ledge tilted back. He did not see how he could lower himself to it, lower himself gently enough to keep from continuing on down the slope. But life or death had narrowed down to this one lean chance, with the probability that even if he could manage it, death would only be delayed. He knew he was close to passing out. He caught the trunk of the tree in his torn right hand, and using the leverage, he began to worm his way back. The trunk was across his diaphragm, then his chest. He hooked his left elbow over it, moved further. When the trunk came under his chin, the almost useless left arm slipped. The trunk hit him under the chin. His feet swung against the rock and he made a thin squeaking sound when his left ankle banged. His right hand began to slip as his weight slowly opened his fingers. But as his hand opened the toes of his right foot touched the ledge. He found precarious balance, and when he let go with his hand, he fell against the cliff face, supported by his right foot. He caught an edge of rock with his right hand as he started to topple. It delayed him slightly, but then he fell full on his back, head snapping back to strike the rock, and the shadow moved quickly over him, the world turning dark.

When he came to, it was a world of blue-gray. He could see the sun on the high peaks across the valley. It took him several moments to decide that it must be nearly night rather than dawn. He watched the sun line move up the peaks. He was thirsty and his body had stiffened. He moved gingerly, painfully, trying to make himself more comfortable. If this was the place to wait for death on this night, then be comfortable, if you can. When the blackness came again, it was not like sleep.

He awoke and stars were high and he felt he was on fire. In the night he babbled and yelled and had strange bright visions. The yells echoed faintly from the far mountain wall of the deep valley. At dawn the visions were gone and he was cold. In the morning there was rain, another heavy rain. He held his face in the rain, and though he did not have enough feeling in his face to know if his mouth was opened or closed, he felt the coolness trickle into his throat and he was able to swallow after a fashion. He pulled his shirt up with his right hand and squeezed the rain moisture from it into his mouth. The water brought him back from the dulled wait for death.

When he was able to look around, he saw that his ledge went narrowly around a shoulder of the cliff, and slanted down slightly. He worked himself over onto his belly. He could use his left elbow, his right hand and arm, his right leg. The left leg dangled. He inched himself along. He did not know how long it took to reach the shoulder of the cliff, one hour or six. There he could see the rest of the ledge. It opened out, almost as wide as a road, and went down steeply. After two hundred yards it reached a place where the mountain side was a different texture. There was a long sand slide, studded with round rocks and boulders. He followed it down with his eyes and saw that it ended at the valley floor where tropic growth was more luxuriant, where a rain-fed stream wound between the great stones that had tumbled down the flanks of the mountains.

The sun baked him, drying the moisture out of him. From the height of the sun he guessed it was early afternoon when he reached the long sand slide. He looked down at the water far below and knew he had to reach it. He looked back the way he had come and he felt pride. He laughed aloud and it was a curious croaking sound. He tried to say Harry Danton's name, but he could not articulate. He sensed the bright edge of delirium again, and fought back to logic and precarious sanity.

If he got onto the sand, he would go down. That was evident. But he could not go feet first. The left leg would crumple under him and turn him and he might roll. If that started, he would roll and bound among the hard stones. There had to be stability in the slide. The left arm had only limited usefulness. He would have to be able to see, and he would need some slightly effective method of steering himself. He thought about it a long time. Finally, with great effort, he tore a strip from his shirt. He crossed his ankles, left ankle across the right, and bound them clumsily. That way the left would not flop loose and dig into the sand. He eased himself out onto the sand slope. He moved slowly at first, head raised, elbows digging in. As he picked up speed he began to move directly toward a large boulder. The top inches of sand slid along with him. He dug the right elbow deeper and it swung him to the right. He almost lost control. He passed the rock so closely it gave his left elbow a sharp painful crack. This was the steering method the bobsledders used. He went faster. He was taking more sand along. The sand flowed over the smaller stones. He yelled in crazy triumph. Then there were more rocks ahead, and these were jagged ones. It was harder to steer. He clawed with his right hand, trying to dig himself sideways. He missed the rocks but he had lost stability. He had turned and began to roll. He rolled violently down the last of the slope, across hard ground, finally came to rest in the heart of a clump of dense shrubbery, unconscious.

In the blue of dusk, in the odd reflected light of the last of the sun on the mountains to the east, he crawled to the brook. He drank until his belly felt tight. He spewed up the water weakly and waited a long time and then drank sparingly. When he knew he would retain it, he crawled into the brush that would protect him from the morning sun.

2

In mid-morning he crawled out and drank. He had expected to feel stronger, but he felt weaker. He rolled onto his back, shaded his eyes, and looked up the dizzy cliff face. He tried to pick out his ledge, but he could not.

I got down from there, he thought. I got down alive. And it would have been a good trick for a whole man. I can tell myself I did that much. I have water and shade. Two ingredients. I need a doctor and food. What is today? It was the ninth of May when they found us. I went over the edge at dawn on the tenth. Yesterday was the eleventh. This will be the twelfth. Sunday morning then. A Sunday in May.

He tried to guess where he was in relation to the smashed car. He closed his eyes and tried to reconstruct how it had looked from the tree. At least it had not burned. It would be wise to get near the car, but not too far from the water. A man on a mountain might spot the car. He might climb down to investigate. There was that frail chance.

It should be in that direction, on the far side of the stream. Two hundred yards, perhaps. Maybe more. I can try it. There's nothing else to do.

He thought for a moment and then his heart began to pound. The car had not burned. Sylvia had liked to keep things in the glove compartment. Cookies, crackers, candy. Her appetite had never softened the trim lines of her body. There would be something there. Enough to give him another day, perhaps. Or two. He began the laborious crawl. He knew it was the only way he could move. Even if he could find a stick and pull himself erect, the bad leg and bad arm were on the same side. If only it could have been the right leg that was bad . . .

From time to time he strained up to see the terrain ahead. When the far bank looked better, he pulled himself through a shallow place in the stream, and took time out to soak himself in a pool a foot and a half deep. Water stung the hurts of his body, the knee and elbows raw with crawling.

On the far bank he found a bush with dark berries. He plucked several and could not decide how he could eat them. His jaw hung slack, badly broken, he knew. He pulped the berries in his fingers, and stuck them into the back of his throat, worked them down with his tongue. They were violently bitter and he coughed them out. The cookies and crackers would be a problem. Perhaps they could be pulped in water, in some sort of container, possibly a hub cap, and drunk like soup.

He moved on under the height of the sun. He stopped when he heard a curious sound, a flapping and croaking sound. He moved toward it. He saw a black ugly bird rise, croaking, tilt creaking wings and soar down again. Another bird came up and went down. He crawled and parted the brush and saw them in an open space, tearing, quarrelling, wings outspread, a tumult of hunger. He closed his eyes when a shift of the wind brought him the sour-sweet smell of what they had been fighting over. When he opened them again he saw, under the moving blackness, the soiled shreds of pistachio green and of yellow. He cawed at them, a furious sound of anger coming from the broken mouth at this ultimate indignity. He hurled small stones and crawled with painful haste. They went away and sat like deacons on the limbs of low barren trees, observing him. He could not look at what was left of Sylvia, could not bring himself to look. They seemed to recognize his weakness, and they moved closer.

For the rest of the afternoon, he worked with the furious energy of insanity. He used the stones close to her first, straining with the heavy ones. But there were not enough. He had to go further away each time, and many times he had to go so far they returned to her, the bolder ones, and he had to drive them away when he came back, pushing the stone along in front of him. He worked through the heat of the day with the mindless determination of a half crippled ant, and he made the cairn bigger and stronger than it had to be made.

Once it was done, his strength ebbed away from him and he lay on his back. The birds seemed to give up; some of them flew away. He watched them work themselves up out of the canyon, laboring up on black wings, circling higher until at last they came into the wind currents off the peaks and circled up there on motionless wings, in evil grace, before gliding off to some unknown place. But there were other birds who waited.

He turned his head and looked at the cairn. He wished he could speak aloud. But he could make the words in his head, and make them so clear he could read them as though he printed them carefully.

"This is a prayer. I have not prayed in many years. It isn't for me. It's for her. Her name was Sylvia. She sinned. She was a beautiful woman. She was twenty-six years old when she died. She died in terror and in shame and in degradation. She paid more than enough during the last hours she had on earth. She had her hell then. She doesn't need any more. Take care of her, somehow. Please."

He crawled to the stream and drank. He knew he could not crawl much farther. He knew the car would have to wait until the next day, if there would be a next day for him. He crawled into the shelter of the brush and lay on his back and watched, through green leaves, the end of the day. And he thought of how she had been in Mexico City.

They had driven down from Juarez in three days. The increasing distance had not given her peace of mind. Rather she had seemed to grow more frightened, day by day, pale, nervous, irritable.

"We're safe now," he told her.

"We'll never be safe. We shouldn't have done it. We shouldn't have tried to do it, Lloyd. We were crazy to try it. We were insane to even think of it. You don't know what they're capable of. You don't know how he'll feel about this. He can't let a thing like this go. We'll never be safe."

"Don't worry about it. Let me take care of things."

"You can't take care of things. You don't understand them. You don't know how they are."

She refused to be calmed. He found a small and inconspicuous hotel in Mexico City, a hotel with a parking lot in the rear where the car would be well concealed. He left the money locked in the trunk compartment. It seemed to be the safest place. He took ten of the hundred dollar bills. He had an idea how such things were managed. She refused to leave the small suite. He went out alone. He knew how careful he had to be. When they had been making plans he had managed to find out, without arousing suspicion, the names of those Latin American countries where citizenship could be arranged. There were three of them. He had no luck with the first consular official. His hints were coldly ignored. At the second place he had luck, even though the man made him uneasy.

The man was named Señor Rillardo, and he had a small unclean office, a look of greed, a rumpled suit, and very small fat white hands.

"You would like to become a citizen of my country?"

"Yes sir."

"It is necessary first to have a visa and then, after you are there, you make application for an immigrante permit.

Then, in two years, if there is approval, after simple tests, you receive first papers. You have a passport?"

"No sir."

"Ah! That makes a problem. What do you have?"

"This. My tourista card."

Rillardo took it and looked at it. "This is your name?"

"Yes, it is."

"You could get a passport, Meester Wescott?"

"I would not care to go back and ask for one. For personal reasons."

"For, perhaps, legal reasons?"

"I am not wanted by the law, Señor Rillardo."

Rillardo spread his small hands and said, "Then?"

"I have an enemy. A very powerful man."

"I see."

"I have understood that . . . in cases of emergency . . . your government is sometimes understanding. Certain shortcuts can be arranged."

Rillardo's face lost all expression. "It is possible. But such things can be very expensive."

"There is some money."

"How much?"

Lloyd smiled. "Isn't that the question I should be asking? Assume there is enough. What can you provide?"

"This is not a promise. I do not commit myself or my . . . associates, Meester Wescott. But if there was enough, this thing could be done. By personal examination and approval I could make of you a citizen of our nation, and I could issue you a passport here. Then air transportation could be most easily arranged. However, this is no guarantee against extradition. We do not offend our very powerful neighbor."

"No one will want to extradite me."

"I can name a figure. You must understand that I must make gifts to very many people. Our small country has a great number of officials. Many of them are men of great probity. For them the gifts must be ample. I would say, for you, it could be done for . . . in American dollars . . . twenty thousand."

"That is too much!"

Rillardo smiled sadly. "Safety is always expensive. Security is a rare commodity in a troubled world, my friend."

Lloyd thought for a moment. "Perhaps, if I were to make you a personal gift, Señor, completely aside from our transaction, it might be that you could talk your friends into a lower figure."

"A gift?"

Lloyd took out the automobile permit issued him when he had crossed the border and handed it to Rillardo. Rillardo pursed his lips. "Such things are difficult. There are Mexican customs to consider. It is not easy."

"Certainly you have friends in the Mexican customs department."

"Acquaintances, only. What is the color of this vehicle?"

"Red and white. A red like the border of that magazine on your desk. As you can see it's a recent model. It has fifteen thousand miles on it. It is a handsome car. I will have no further use for it . . . if we should have a meeting of the minds."

Rillardo laid the permit on his desk. "And what do you think would be a fair figure, Meester Wescott, for what you wish me to do for you?"

"May I first ask a question? If one lives quietly in your country, how much does it cost to live there, in American dollars?"

"Quietly? I must have more information."

"A small rented house not too far from a city. A full time maid and gardener. Good food. Perhaps a small swimming pool. Very little entertaining. Reasonably modern utilities."

"For that . . . for a man alone, I should say it could be done adequately, even with a certain style, for twenty-five hundred dollars a year."

Lloyd did a rapid computation. Say three thousand a year for two. Twenty from a hundred and ten would leave ninety. Thirty years.

"This is my offer, Señor Rillardo. I will pay the twenty thousand you ask. In cash."

The black eyebrows went up. "I do not understand?"

"For both of us. There are two of us. Here is her tourista card."

Rillardo took it and read the name aloud. "Miss Sylvia Kennedy. This is difficult. You make it difficult for me. Can you not be husband and wife?"

"Not legally. You can call us that, if you wish."

"I see. She was the woman of the man you speak of?"

"His wife. She used her birth certificate to get her card. She walked across the bridge."

"Perhaps you took the money of this man too?"

"That should not concern you, Señor."

"You are correct. I must apologize."

"Can it be done?"

Rillardo thought for a long time, frowning, fingering the corner of the auto permit. He smiled. "I can do it. But she must be called your wife."

"All right. What's the next step?"

"I must have ten thousand American dollars. I can issue the passport in two weeks time. There are certain things that must be checked first."

"Can you give me a receipt?"

"Of course not! That is absurd!"

"I will give you five thousand. I will give you the final amount when we board the plane."

"You make it more difficult."

"I am sorry."

Rillardo sighed heavily. "Then I shall arrange it your way. Have you the money here?"

"I will bring it to you."

"Today, please."

He took the five thousand back to Rillardo. The man counted it carefully, licking his white thumb. He folded it casually and put it in his inside jacket pocket.

"Two weeks from this day," he said. "That will be the seventeenth of May. A Friday. Reservations will be arranged for you and I will have the tickets here."

After he was standing again, Lloyd said, "We do not want to stay here in the city. We may be taking a chance to stay here. Can you suggest where we could go?"

Rillardo suggested they drive north on the Inter-American Highway to Zimapan and there turn west on the new road into the mountainous province of Queretaro. He was certain they could find a quiet place to stay.

On the way back to the hotel Lloyd felt entirely unreal. He felt as though he were taking a part in a half-forgotten movie. This was certainly not what his life had prepared him for—flight into a foreign land with another man's wife and money, dickering in a shabby office for illegal passports. He and Sylvia were to appear with pictures to be pasted on those purchased documents, sealed with the great seal of the nation of exile.

He was not so naive as to think it could go off without a hitch. There was the possibility that Rillardo would find the task too difficult. Then he would deny ever having seen Lloyd or having taken the five thousand. And there would be no way to prove it.

Or, it might be a private plane, and after the balance of the money had been taken from them, they might be dropped into the sea. Rillardo knew Lloyd had money, and knew Lloyd could not turn to his own government for help. Many risks could be taken to acquire the money of a helpless man. And Rillardo had an unsavory look about him.

Yet Lloyd was determined to make Sylvia feel that it was working out perfectly. That evening she had made him tell her over and over again how it would be for them, how they would be safe. She clung to him as though he was her last chance in all the world.

That night they left the city after dark and stayed in a hotel cottage in Zimapan. He had purchased Scotch. Sylvia drank until she was incoherent, until she passed out. He had never seen her drink so heavily. He was more than a little drunk himself. Her fear was infectious. He stood over the bed and looked down at the spill of dark hair, heard her thick breathing. This was not like the magic in the beginning. This had become furtive and sordid. He even thought of leaving her with half the money and driving hard for the border, crossing at, say, Matamoros into Brownsville, and trying to lose himself in the states. But he knew he could never leave her. It was a curious twisted love, but it was strong, and he could not leave her.

He sat and brooded for a long time. He became very depressed. He was certain that, somehow, they were going to be robbed and left penniless in Mexico. Rillardo would arrange it somehow. He was a fool to carry it all around in one chunk. It should be spread out. That would provide a reserve. He gave it intent alcoholic consideration. He remembered the jar in the car, a wide-mouthed glass jar with a screw lid. It contained what was left of the peanut brittle Sylvia had bought at the gas station in Las Cruces. The car was beside the cottage. He got the jar and dumped the candy out. He took the money from the trunk compartment into the cottage. It was in a blue canvas gym bag. He had owned the zipper bag for a long time. Once upon a time he had used it to carry basketball gear in.

By wadding the bigger bills tightly, he was able to get forty thousand into the jar. That left about sixty-five in cash. If everything worked out, he would be able to come back one day and get the forty thousand. And if it didn't work out at all, the forty thousand would be a reserve for them. He felt very clever. He wanted to wake Sylvia up and explain to her how cleverly he was handling everything. He had thought of burying it in the ground. He looked around the cottage. The walls were paneled. He went out and got the tire iron. He chose a spot where the bathroom door opened against a wall of the bedroom. There were no light outlets there. He carefully pried off the quarter round, then pried one panel board loose at the floor level and pulled it back, yet not so far back it would pull the top molding free. The jar sat neatly on one of the cross joists, and seeing that it was exactly the right size made him feel his plan was more valid. He nailed the board and the molding back, using a towel to keep from marring the wood. The cottages were quite new. There was no reason why it should be disturbed for years. He put everything away and went to bed.

He did not remember hiding the money until he was thirty miles west of Zimapan, on the new road. Sylvia was surly and sullen with the pangs of hangover. When he told her about it, she reacted violently and they had a bitter quarrel, the worst quarrel yet. Finally he got her to admit the wisdom of what he had done.

The new road dipped close to the village of Talascatan and then climbed gently up the heart of a valley for a mile and a half, to the Montañas Motel, a new place on a hill overlooking the highway. It was secluded. Cars beside the units could not be seen from the road. The units were set very far apart. The sign said in Spanish and English that there were cooking facilities.

They stopped and the quarrel was forgotten. Their unit was at the end the farthest from the others. The owners were Swiss, a gentle couple who had lived in Mexico for many years, and who had managed a hotel at Acapulco until it was torn down to make room for a more flamboyant structure. They had saved their money, had speculated in oceanfront land, and had made enough to build this motel. They said business was slow because the road was new. Next year the new road would join the secondary road that ran from Rio Verde to San Luis Potosi, and there would then be a great deal of through traffic.

Lloyd registered as Mr. and Mrs. Wesley Floyd. Their unit was clean and new. There were two large double beds in the bedroom, a cot in the small living room. That night, in the barranca behind the motel, the insects made a night-long shrilling. She lay in his arms and whispered, "I think it's going to be all right, Lloyd darling. Tonight for the first time, I think we will . . . be safe."

During the days they toasted in the sun behind the motel. In the evenings they walked down to Talascatan and sat at one of the tables in front of a small restaurant and cantina facing the square and watched the young people walk around and around the square with the stained fountain and grubby bandstand. They drank the dark strong beer called Dos Equis, and they ate great bowls of rich caldo gallego, and later walked hand in hand through the night, walked back to the Montañas Motel, slightly drunk on the beer, hand in hand and singing softly in the night. On those few nights it seemed to him that what they had done was both good and necessary. A marriage to Harry Danton could not be called a marriage. This woman was his now, and would be forever his.

They walked back on the night of the ninth and the stars were very clear and high. They walked by all the other units to their own place where there was a starlight gleam on the bumper of the Pontiac parked behind it, under their bedroom windows.

He unlocked the door and she went in first and the lights went on. Sylvia screamed once. Perhaps she screamed again, but by that time the portable radio was on at full volume. Lloyd had tried to fight Tulsa with his fists. Tulsa, grinning and clowning, had worked him back into a corner, wedged him there, big shoulder under Lloyd's chin holding him upright, while he ripped his big hands into Lloyd's middle, working him the way a fighter in training works the heavy bag. He worked him until Lloyd's arms flapped loose as empty sleeves, until his chin bounced idiotically on Tulsa's shoulder, teeth clicking, room bouncing in his dazed vision. Then Tulsa backed off, held his left palm flat against Lloyd's chest, chopped him three times in the face with an overhand right. With the last blow the room bulged, turned red, and collapsed around him like a tent.

When he came to, he was in a cane arm chair, hands tied together behind the chair, mouth wedged full of cloth. The door was ajar and he could hear voices out there, hear the Swiss talking to a stranger in Spanish. His chair was shoved over into a corner. Tulsa stood listening. Benny stood behind Sylvia, holding her close to him with one thick arm around her slim waist, a grimy hand flat across her mouth. Sylvia's black hair was tangled, her eyes wide and hot and furious.

The voices stopped and Valerez came into the room and shut the door. "He go now," Valerez said in clumsy English.

"What did he want?" Tulsa asked.

"Too many peoples he said for one place so it is more. I give him eight pesos."

Tulsa shrugged. He went to each of the three windows, checked to make certain the blinds were completely closed. He paused in front of Lloyd, lifted his chin up, looked down at him. "Good morning, baby! Had a nice little vacation? Had a nice honeymoon? Wait a minute! Hell, she's still married to Harry, so what do you call it? Couldn't be a honeymoon, now could it? You're a bright one, baby. If you wanted action, you should have done something not so risky. Like maybe jumping off the hotel roof."

Sylvia began to kick and writhe. Benny cursed her. Tulsa said, "Quiet the bitch down, Benny."

Benny spun her violently, hit her with one quick clean motion, and the noise of the blow was small and brutal. He caught her as she fell forward and grinned at Tulsa, evil and meaningful grin on the clown face. "Where at you want her, Tuls?"

"In the bedroom. Then we hunt the money."

They found it easily. Tulsa brought it in, pulled the table over under a light, dumped it out. Benny sat down and counted it with the professional skill of a bank teller, jotting down totals for each stack, packing the stacks neatly in the zipper bag. He totaled his figures and said, "Sixty-four thousand eight hundred and ten, Tulsa. It's supposed to be more than that, isn't it?"

"Harry couldn't tell for sure. You know how it is. They'd claim more anyhow, wouldn't they? Giz, keep an eye on the dish."

"Dish?" Valerez said, looking around helplessly.

"Watch the girl, stupid! And just watch her, nothing else."

Then they turned the radio up again. Tulsa took off his shirt. They took the gag out of Lloyd's mouth. He had felt pain before. Not this kind of pain. This was a white light that kept exploding in his head. When he bucked in the chair and tried to scream, Benny would clap the towel over his mouth. Lloyd knew he fainted, but he did not know how many times. He would have told a dozen times had the pain been smaller. But the pain came in bursts that prevented his speaking. And when the pain faded, a dull stubborn anger closed his mouth. "That's all there was," he would bellow. He shouted it a dozen times.

Tulsa finally straightened up, dropped the cigar, turned his foot on it. "I'll buy it, Benny. Stuff his mouth again. And go get that tequila."

"Aren't we going soon?"

Tulsa looked at his watch. Benny tied the gag roughly in place. Tulsa said, "We kill time. Valerez says we can find a good place not too far, but not in the dark. So we leave about four. It's after ten now."

Lloyd sat with his chin on his chest, the tears running out of his eyes, breathing hard, sobbing against the gag. He could smell the rich stink of his burned chest and belly, his burned feet. He knew he could never be the same person again. He knew he could not go back to what he had been before. He had learned, abruptly, a special kind of hatred. He thought he could not hate any more violently than he did in those moments. Yet an hour later the hatred was stronger. The next hour tempered it, like a cherry red blade thrust into the quenching oil.

"She wants come out!" Valerez called in a nervous tone.

"So let her come," Tulsa said.

Sylvia appeared in the doorway. Her jaw was bruised. But she stood proudly, her head up, her eyes furious. She looked beyond Tulsa and Benny at Lloyd and her face changed. She tried to come to him, and Benny thrust her back roughly. "Lloyd, darling!" she said. "What did you two do to him?"

Benny burlesqued shyness, rubbing the side of his foot on the floor. "Well, we had a sort of like a cook out."

"You filthy monsters," she said, and her eyes filled with tears. She looked at Tulsa. "Are you taking me back to Harry?"

"Harry don't want to have to look at you, Mrs. Danton. Harry all of a sudden got tired of you, like."

Lloyd saw her bite her lip, glance toward the blue

bag. "You've got the money. Why don't you go and leave us alone now. You've done enough to Lloyd."

Tulsa spoke patiently to her, an explanatory tone. "Harry wouldn't much like that. He said you should have a real hard time. Most of all you, Mrs. Danton. A worse time than Lloyd darling here on account of he didn't know the score as good as you know it."

She looked at him with spirit and with bravery. "All right, Tulsa. Beat me up. Or should Benny hold me?"

She wore the pale blue linen dress he had bought her in Mexico City, at the shop on Juarez when her terror was so great she would not leave the hotel. Tulsa reached out with one hand. She tried to move back, but he caught the square neck of the dress and ripped down. He tore out the entire front of it. What was left of the dress hung from one shoulder. He plucked it off and tore away the wisps of nylon. She tried to cover herself and then let her hands drop slowly to her sides. Some of the courage was gone, some of the spirit. She kept her chin up, her eyes fixed on Tulsa, but her mouth trembled.

Benny made a grunt of appreciation. Tulsa said, "You look maybe a little better than I guessed, Mrs. Danton. Scared?"

"What . . . what are you going to do?"

"Right now? Get a drink. You stand right there, Mrs. Danton. Hell, you're a lot better than a pinup. More real. You want a drink?"

"No."

"Seriously, Mrs. Danton, that's the only break I'm giving you. Harry wouldn't like me doing this, giving you a drink. You want to know how it goes? You got yourself killed. When you and Lloyd darling were twenty miles outside of Oasis Springs, you were a dead girl. Didn't you know?"

"Can't you . . ."

"Not with Harry giving the orders, I can't. You're just as dead as Lloyd darling. You're standing there dead. Now you want a drink?"

Her eyes were staring. She looked at Lloyd and through him. "Yes," she whispered.

Benny brought Tulsa the glass and the bottle he had just opened. Tulsa poured the glass more than half full of tequila. She sipped it. Lloyd stared at Valerez. The man looked uncomfortable, embarrassed. Benny glanced at Sylvia greedily.

"Hurry it up," Tulsa said.

She gulped and coughed and gulped again. Her face looked dulled, her eyes glazed, her complexion grayish. There was sweat on her face and shoulders and breasts. She finished the last of the tequila. Tulsa took the glass from her, threw it to Benny. Benny caught it deftly. Tulsa pushed the girl back into the bedroom and closed the door behind the two of them.

Lloyd stared incredulously, with a sick horror, at the closed bedroom door. He shut his eyes hard upon the scene in his mind, but he could not blot it out. Benny pulled his chair—the chair with Lloyd in it—over to the table.

"Join the party," Benny said cheerfully. "You keep sitting around in corners with your mouth shut, people won't like you. You know how to play gin, Giz? Good! You got some competition." Benny slapped the cards on the table and fanned them. He leaned close to Lloyd, winked in a jovial, insinuating way, jerked his thumb toward the closed bedroom door and said, "Little card game keeps a fella's mind off stuff and things. My deal."

Benny dealt deftly, picked up his hands, brows knotted, lips moving as he read off his cards to himself. The radio had been tuned low, so low the hillbilly music from Texas was but barely audible. Lloyd looked at Benny and recognized the expression on his face. It was the same expression he had seen so many times when Benny sat reading one of his comic books. Benny specialized in the fantasy comic books, full of slimed monsters, leggy girls in space suits, young scientist heroes and death rays. Lloyd remembered all the times he had forced himself to endure patiently Benny's retelling of one of the plots, little squat Benny with his lumpy clown face, wriggling with intensity, exuding a fine spray of spittle when he came to the most dramatic parts. He had heard that Benny Bernholz was one of Harry Danton's most reliable and efficient hoodlums, but that did not seem credible. He remembered how Benny had become fascinated with the way the landscape architects were turning the raw land around the Hotel Green Oasis into a tropical garden, how he annoyed the workmen with countless questions. Later, Harry Danton had let Benny take sole responsibility for a large formal flower bed to the east of the hotel, between the Olympic pool and the Copper Casino. Benny haunted the garden supply store down in the village of Oasis Springs, had struggled through the terminology of dozens of catalogues. The flower bed had been a masterpiece. Benny had made an event out of each new bloom, a disaster out of any hint of blight. No tourist could take a photograph of the large flower bed without Benny quickly sidling into the scene, chest inflated, carefully casual, his lesser version of a Durante nose as red as his bald spot from the long hours in the desert sun.

It was easier to picture Tulsa in the role of hired assassin, yet even that had not seemed plausible a thousand years ago when he and Tulsa had played gin at odd moments, when he and Tulsa had gone out into the big kitchens when the skeleton night staff was on and had made the thick sandwiches of tongue and imported cheese and rare roast beef. Tulsa's last name was Haynes, and he was from Oklahoma and he was half Indian. His shoulders were so broad that at a distance he looked much shorter than his six feet. Lloyd had seen him, on a drunken wager, plant his feet, stand with his back to the hood, squat so he could grasp the bumper, and lift the front wheels of a Buick clear of the ground.

Lloyd had felt he was close to them, friendly with them. In the chain of command, as hotel manager, he was their superior. Almost, but not quite. Harry Danton had said, "Use the boys when you can, Lloyd. I'd rather have you keeping them busy than have Charlie trying to use them." Charlie Bliss was in charge of the gambling end and worked with Harry Danton on the entertainment.

But, with both Benny and Tulsa, there was a curious reserve he could not penetrate. He was not quite one of the club. Sometimes he felt they came very close to patronizing him. Benny and Tulsa would go off on unexplained missions, sometimes alone, sometimes together, for as long as two weeks, though usually for only a day or two. Once when Tulsa came back, Lloyd made the mistake of asking him where he had been. Tulsa looked at him without any expression and said, "I've been to London to see the queen." Lloyd didn't ask again. He knew that the Hotel Green Oasis was but one phase of Harry Danton's operations, and that for various reasons Harry had chosen it as his headquarters. There were often special guests who had to be given rooms, the best suites, regardless of the reservation picture. These men generally drank and ate in their suites, spent hours in conferences with Harry, and seldom appeared in the Copper Casino. One of them, a small grey man without hair, eyebrows or lashes, registered often as J. Baron. Harry Danton treated him with respect bordering on servility, and had instructed Lloyd to see personally that Mr. Baron received top service. Each time Baron was in the house, Charlie Bliss had to move a silver dollar slot up to his suite after having a mechanic drop the 60-40 odds back to 50-50.

He had known Benny and known Tulsa, and now he knew that he had not known them at all, nor had he known Harry Danton. These men had been outside the range of his experience, and beyond his ability to project an awareness of evil. But now he had a new appreciation of them. Now he had seen them on the job. Now he knew their value to Harry. Any man without heart or conscience, with only ruthlessness and cruelty, can be invaluable to the Harry Dantons.

Lloyd sat tied in the chair. The script was wrong. There were always the good guys and the bad guys. And the beautiful woman. Lloyd had known all his life that he was one of the good guys. That made it simple, because then you always knew how it came out. The good guy and the beautiful girl would always get into one hell of a mess, but something always happened just at the very last minute, just when they both seemed doomed. Something happened. The bonds were worked loose, and you felled the bad guys with a chair. Or the cops came. Or the cavalry. It usually happened just when they were getting set to torture you. But something was wrong with this script and they went right ahead and did it. It didn't happen in the nick of time. The nick of time went right on by while you screamed and screamed onto a bloody towel. And always the beautiful girl was threatened by a fate worse than death. And they never quite got to her. They made some error in timing, or they left a gun around loose. But this nick of time went right on by too. So you sat and watched a game of rummy and you looked hard at the cards in Benny's hand and the cards he drew so you could take your mind away from the crawling horrors behind a locked door.

Tulsa came out of the bedroom, buckling his belt. He left the door open. He looked casually at Lloyd, and stood behind Benny, looking down into his hand. Benny drew the ten of spades, went down with four and caught Valerez with twenty-three count.

"Take it from here," Benny said. "It's no blitz. He lucked out on me two hands ago." He got up and Tulsa took his chair. "How is it, Tuls?" he asked.

"She ain't what anybody'd call cooperative," Tulsa said.

"Me, I got enough cooperation for two." He swaggered over to the door, hitching his pants up. He knocked on the door frame and cooed, "Oh darling! Are you decent?"

He went in and shut the door. Tulsa and Valerez played cards. They drank tequila. Lloyd saw a mosquito land on Tulsa's shoulder. The muscles quivered like the hide of a horse and the insect whined away. He looked at Tulsa's thick brown neck and thought of knives. Valerez went gin three times in a row and Tulsa scowled with annoyance. As far as the two men were concerned, Lloyd did not seem to exist. Benny came out, burlesquing extreme exhaustion. He kibitzed until the game was finished. Then Valerez looked inquiringly at Tulsa.

"Go ahead," Tulsa said. He went quickly. When the door had closed behind him, Benny said, "They like to get hold of a white woman. He'd like it better if she was blonde."

"Was she still crying?" Tulsa asked.

"No. She's like a zombie. Your deal, Tuls. Say, there's a pretty smart operator, that spic."

"He found 'em quick."

"You don't give me any more cards than he did. Want to make this a half buck a point?"

"Sure. After this game."

"Wise guy," Benny muttered and put down a cold hand for gin.

Valerez came out, pulled another chair over, and combed his hair straight back with a small green comb. He gave Lloyd a quick nervous glance. They started a three-handed game at higher stakes. They played for an hour. Tulsa went back into the bedroom. After he came out, Benny went in. Then he came hurrying right back out, rigid with indignation.

"Chrissake, Tuls. She's dead! You killed her! What the hell did you do? Her face is all dark like."

Tulsa flexed one big hand in a descriptive gesture.

"What the hell for?" Benny demanded.

"You want to say goodby or something? I said goodby, for you and me and Giz and Harry and Lloyd darling and all the folks back home."

Benny sat down and looked petulantly at Tulsa. "You know, sometimes you give me the God damn creeps, you thick-headed Indian."

"You want in the game or don't you?"

Benny sighed. "So deal me in. How much longer we got?"

Tulsa looked at his watch. "An hour."

"Want I should get a fresh bottle outa the car?"

"No more drinks."

The gag made Lloyd's jaws ache. He watched the three of them and thought of all the ways he could kill them, all the ways he would enjoy. The chair back cut into his upper arms. His arms were numb from there on down.

Finally Tulsa said, "Go put clothes on her, Benny."

"Hey, Tuls! Honest! I can't touch nothing like that."

Tulsa put his cards down. "She's gotta have clothes on. So go dress her. Now!"

Benny mumbled, whined but obeyed. He came to the bedroom door and said in a surly voice, "So she's dressed. Now what?"

"Now put her in the Pontiac."

"She's too heavy."

Tulsa cursed and got up. Lloyd watched him carry her out of the bedroom. He got one look at her dead face. Her right eye had been hammered shut. It was knotted like blue grapes.

And then there had been the ride up out of the night of the valley into the dawn of the mountains.

He lay on his back and the small leaves of the brush made a pattern against the stars. The wind changed. A whisper of breeze carried the scent of decay to his nostrils. He heard a dog bark, very far away. The stream made a hurrying sound close by. A few insects made a thin and endless screaming.

Tulsa, Benny, Valerez, Harry. I'll get out of here. Somehow I'll get out of here.

3

From then on there was no coherence to thought or memory. There was blazing sun, a memory of the car, crumpled as though it had been wadded in a fist, and beginning to rust. There was a pasty mess in a hub cap and he tried to swallow it. There were the birds waiting. Then he burned, and he made his croaking shouts and he listened for the inhuman echo. There was rain, and pain, and the heat of fever, and all kinds of curious things that came to him, Harry stepping carefully over the stones, Sylvia clinging to his arm, both of them smiling as they came toward him, and on their shoulders were perched the black vultures, riding easily there.

Then he was face down and something carried him along, lurching with him, something with shaggy brown hair and small hooves. Much later there was a dark and smoky place and hard hands holding him down as he screamed and screamed.

Everything was twisted and distorted, without continuity or meaningfulness—bright flashes and long patches of blackness. It was like a storm that passed over and through him and faded away down a valley.

By turning his head to the left he could see the bright irregular oblong of the door, the sunlight outside. He lay on a rustling softness, close to the floor, and the floor was of packed dirt. He liked to look out. He could see the side of a hill, and a wedge of sky. The hill was cultivated. Sometimes he could see people working in that incredibly steep field.

When the light was right, when it was late in the day, the sun walked slowly in across the dirt floor. It never quite reached him. Before it reached him, the sun dropped behind a mountain. When it was closest he could reach out and touch the edge of the sunlight. It was a long time before he had strength to do that. His hands were too heavy to lift. When the light was strongest, he often looked at his hands. They were pale and trembling and skeletal. His wrists were like stalks. The right palm was deeply scarred. The left wrist was lumpy, and had but limited movement. The fingers worked. The wrist would bend forward, but he could not move it from side to side.

He often felt of his face. His lower jaw was tied in place. It felt like a piece of rawhide that passed under his chin, over the top of his head. There was no familiarity in the contours under his fingertips. He was heavily bearded, yet there were shiny places where the beard did not grow. His nose felt like a withered button, and the left side of his face felt strangely hollow. His tongue explored the splintered stubs of teeth, finding the sharp places, lingering there.

At night six of them slept in the small square room and an adjoining room. They cooked there, on a sheet of metal over charcoal. There was an old lantern lighted only on special occasions. Smoke found its own way out a hole in the thatched roof. Sometimes, when the wind was wrong, they all coughed and choked. It seemed a long time before he could tell them apart clearly, or isolate their names out of the babble of conversation. For a long time he had not had the energy to try, but as the life trickled slowly back into him, and as his mind came alive, he began to listen for the names, try to figure out the relationships, try to pick up words and phrases of their conversation. There were three children, three boys. Pepe was about twelve, Armandito about eight, Felipe about six. They were happy children, with wide brown almost identical faces. They would often come and look down upon him with solemn unwinking curiosity.

The man of the house was named Armando, a squat brown man with a look of leathery toughness, a shock of startlingly white hair. His woman, the mother of the boys, was Concha who was perhaps thirty, perhaps twenty years younger than Armando, a placid heavy woman who sometimes fed him, spooning soups and thick pastes through the gap where teeth had been, holding him up gently when she held the pottery cup of cold water to his lips, washing his body with brusque efficiency in which there was a leavening of tenderness.

Usually it was the girl who took care of him. Her name was Isabella, and often they called her 'Bella or 'Bellita. She seemed to be seventeen or eighteen, a sturdy girl with a broad brown face in which he saw a family resemblance to the three boys, with black thick brows, black braided hair coarse and shiny as the tail hair of a black horse. She came to feed him and care for his needs during the day when the others worked, came to him smelling of sun and the fields and of sweat, impersonally gentle, sometimes crooning to him with the reassuring sounds you make to a small child. He knew she was not directly of this family, yet somehow related. She called Concha Tia, and Armando Tio. It was Isabella who taught the small boys. She made them drone lessons in unison, and she made them draw letters in the packed dirt outside the room with a pointed stick.

Other people often came to the rooms and there was much talk. And much laughter. And often music and singing. These were poor people, he knew. They worked very hard. Their life had a certain cadence of love. Many times other women, two or three, would come to visit Concha. They would bring flat stones and stone rollers and they would sit for tireless hours on the floor, cross-legged, grinding corn. With water and lime water they would turn the white powder into a paste, then slap it into tortillas. The slapping sounds merged with the sun and the sleepy afternoon, and their light quick voices as they worked and talked.

They were a clean people. He could hear the sound of falling water not far away. They used a coarse soap. Isabella sometimes wore her braids in coronet fashion. Other times the two long braids dangled. Sometimes when she bent over him, one of the coarse gleaming ropes would fall across his face, smelling of sun and freshness and the strong soap. There were goats that sometimes came and peered in at the door. When the wary scrawny chickens wandered in, Concha would flap her skirts and chase them out.

For a long time he was aware only of such a complete weariness, such an utter exhaustion, that he could not do anything for himself, nor could he concentrate long on what went on around him. His attention span was as short as that of a small child, and he slept often. He did not try to speak. In sleep he did not dream.

Then, when the days were very warm, he began to take an interest in things around him, and began to do more for himself. When he hitched himself up into a half-sitting position and reached for the bowl, Isabella let him feed himself until, half-way through, his hands and arms became too weary. It was then that he began to